Eddie King FRSA is an author, copywriter, and television presenter.

Born and raised in Hampstead, London, he spent many years working in the film industry as a producer and script consultant on large-budget Hollywood productions. He is a prominent ambassador of American country music across Europe, and co-hosts a weekly primetime television series. He currently splits his time between London, Los Angeles, and Nashville.

Eddie has written five novels, all in the contemporary romance genre. 'Spoilt For Choice' earned him a Young Writers' Award nomination and 'Southern Girl: Daisy Dukes and Cowboy Boots' has been adapted for screen.

To find out more about him and his career, follow him on Facebook, Twitter, and Instagram.

 /kingsays      @kingsays      @eddieleeking

# The Lost Romantics

Eddie King

Parakeet
Publishing

First published in Great Britain in 2020
by Parakeet Publishing
This paperback edition published in 2020
Available as an eBook from June 2020

Parakeet Publishing, London
www.parakeetpublishing.com

A CIP catalogue record for this book is available from the British Library.

ISBN: 978-0-9935032-4-5

Printed and bound in Great Britain

Other books by Eddie King include:

Worst First Kiss
ISBN: 978-0-9935032-2-1

Southern Girl: Daisy Dukes and Cowboy Boots
ISBN: 978-0-9935032-0-7

*For the girl that took a chance*

*on me and swiped right.*

# MAX

"So, let me set the scene for you. There I was, standing in front of one of my favourite Gerhard Richters at the Tate Modern, filled with sheer marvel and, perhaps, a little envy. Most of the gallerygoers either walked straight through, discounting the four giant masterpieces on the wall, or did the obligatory lap of the room on their way to the gift shop, but she came and stood right next to me to appreciate the carefully concocted chaos on the canvas in front of us. We must have stood there, side by side, for a good ten minutes before I conjured up the courage to say something. I was there first, so, technically, I wasn't being a creep. I commented on how powerful that particular piece was, or some rubbish like that, but she completely blanked me. I turned to face her and saw a single tear trickle down her rosy cheek. I handed her the handkerchief from my breast pocket and waited a few beats before quipping that thirty million pounds for a bit of paint scattered around a piece of cotton in no orderly fashion sometimes made me cry, too. She burst out a single snort, maybe slightly too loudly for a gallery, which I took as my cue to introduce myself—"

"Bull-scheisse!" yelled Hugo from across the table. You know how those cool American kids sometimes substituted Spanish words into their everyday vocabulary? Well, Hugo started doing it with German, ever since he took one of those 23andMe DNA family heritage tests and found out that his great-great-something-or-other was once upon a time somewhere in line for the German throne. You would never have known it from his thick brown curls, year-round Mediterranean tan, meticulously maintained designer stubble, and olive oil charm. He might have been the most traditionally good-looking one of our group, but he definitely wasn't always the luckiest when it came to women. "You had me until the whole hanky in the blazer pocket," he admitted.

Fair enough. Maybe I took it a little too far, but that would have been pretty smooth.

"What a fagoli," Cali wisecracked in a ghastly New Jersey accent as he reached over to my stack and threw a couple of chips into the middle.

Apparently, I was big blind again and Cali had been watching reruns of *The Sopranos*. I know, I know, poker night with the boys was so 2010, but we made a pact back then that if we were all in town, we'd meet up for a night of cards, whiskey, and cigars on the first Monday of every month. We may have ditched the cigars soon after we realised that none of us actually liked them and that they made our clothes stink the next morning, but the rest had become a tradition that no one dared to break.

The action, if you could call it that, was on Will, and I had a tenner saying that he'd fold. He was a very... conservative player, shall we say. He thought long and hard, looked at his hand several times, calculated his odds, and then surprised us all by calling. Cali, who should have folded knowing that Will was only ever in when he was sitting on a monster, instead, as usual, came in with an aggressive raise. I was sitting on pocket Aces, so, "I re-raise."

"I see the meet-cute wasn't your only bluff," Cali teased. "Well, where did you actually meet her?"

"I was in Waitrose, you know, the nice one in Belgravia, doing my big weekly shop last Friday night. As I turned out of the biscuit aisle, our trolleys collided. I apologised, but she just smiled and rolled in the opposite direction before I had a chance to strike up a conversation. I deliberately crossed paths with her a few times throughout the store, hoping to get another smile. Conscious that my usual cans of Coke, Kit Kats, and ketchup made me look like a 10-year-old, I opted for elderflower lemonade, several bags of fruit, and a red onion chutney that will most likely expire in my fridge. I timed my final stop at the wine section perfectly. We stood there reading all the labels and then both reached for the last bottle of Montepulciano d'Abrazzo. Our hands touched and our eyes met. She offered it to me, I offered it to her, she offered it to me again, and then I boldly took a shot and suggested that we share it over the matching Charlie Bigham's ready meals we had in our trolleys. We walked back along the river, hand in hand — "

"And what river is that? The world-famous Knightsbridge River?" Cali asked as he dealt the final card.

"The river that just gave me an Ace-high flush," I said smugly as I flipped over my cards and swept up all the chips from the middle. Confused, followed by frustrated, Will threw in his hand. I continued, "Fine, maybe even I didn't believe that one. Truth is, I was sitting on the toilet and I swiped right. Happy? Who said romance was dead?"

"Alas, the forgotten days of handwritten love letters, candlelit dinners, and mix CDs," mourned Will.

"Yep, now it's all about ghosting, zombieing, breadcrumbing, and laybying," I added.

Will was proudly oblivious to modern life. "I spend half of my time looking up abbreviations and the other half deciphering emojis," he complained. "For ages, I wondered why everyone was suddenly so obsessed with Ireland, but then I found out that IRL means *In Real Life*. And what the bloody hell does a peach have to do with anything? Now, what's all this fairytale stuff?"

Hugo demystified, "Ghosting is when you cut off all communication without any warning. Zombieing is when you resurface — come back from the dead, as it were — after a period of ghosting. I'm guessing, simply by the name, that breadcrumbing is when you send intermittent messages to lead someone on just to keep it alive, but even I have absolutely no idea what laybying is."

"It's when you date someone who is okay, but you keep your profiles active and continue to flirt with better options in the hopes of an upgrade," I explained

"Horrific!" Will howled.

"It's what I do with Hugo's mum," Cali roasted.

"Really, a *your mum* joke? What are we, twelve years old?" Hugo sighed.

I thought it was still funny.

The game fizzled out a few hands after Will, the guy who managed millions of pounds for some of London's most elite businessmen, and more worryingly, gave us all financial advice, was dead in the water. We didn't feel too bad for him though because he earned more than all of us. Well, technically, Cali made the most money from the property portfolio his father gifted him on the day of our graduation, but the business card he slipped girls in clubs read, "retired," and the fact that he'd never actually done a day of real work in his life, meant that it didn't count. Now, if we were talking potential, Hugo was way out in front. Will would tap out at a mil in salary and maybe a couple more in bonuses, Cali's lack of ambition kept him in place, and I, for some reason, chose to follow my dream and become an artist. Sure, one day, most likely after my death, one of my paintings might sell for a bit, or sell at all, but Hugo, Hugo was in the right space at the right time. He founded a tech incubator called VIRALARM—an anagram of Virtual Reality, Artificial Intelligence, Augmented Reality, and Machine Learning. Genius! Much to his dissatisfaction though, Cali called it FIRE ALARM and constantly pitched him awful app ideas. My favourite of his was a gay dating app called Cockatoo—only because it sounded like a cock-or-two. Also genius.

Cali was gearing up to kick us out of his suite, but Will and I were enjoying reminiscing of a simpler time. A time when two blue ticks didn't mean anything, a time when a single Facebook post couldn't make or break your day, and a time when you didn't have to dream up fanciful fantasies of how you met the love of your life. Was I looking through rose-coloured-glasses? Maybe, but I'd had enough. I had sworn off social media just as often as I swore off alcohol after a heavy night out, but those damn TikTok videos got me back every time. "Let's fight back. Let's go back to doing things like we used to. Let's start a movement. Let's bring romance back," I preached. I held my thumb in the air, "Look at it. I've been swiping so much, it hurts. I have Tinder thumb."

"Why don't you just swipe less then?" Will interrupted, unenthusiastically.

"It's not that simple. It's an illness. A disease. A condition. When I'm on my phone, I lose track of everything around me and go into autopilot, swiping for hours.

Sometimes, I open Instagram straight after I just closed it. Together, we can do this." As I picked up the spirit in my promise to resist, I looked for support that just wasn't there. Will chose not to subscribe to any of that malarkey in the first place, Hugo used his work as an excuse, and Cali couldn't have been more disinterested in the conversation.

"Are you bringing Tinder girl to my party tomorrow night?" he asked.

Damn! To hide the fact that I'd forgotten all about it, I challenged, "First, for your information, it's Bumble girl, thank you very much. She does have some class. Second, why would anyone throw a birthday party on a Tuesday night?"

"Well, that's the day my birthday is on," he started. He should have also finished on what was a good point, but in true Cali fashion, he had to continue until he ruined it, "And Tuesday is the best night to go out because the riffraff all have jobs to go to on Wednesday morning, so the clubs aren't filled with Ben Shermans." Ben Shermans — an antiquated term for yobs who used to put on their finest pastel-coloured Ben Sherman shirts and hit the town on Friday and Saturday nights.

Will stood up, shook his head, grabbed his jacket, and made for the exit. As much as we all cringed by the way Cali framed it, the fact remained that we did all have the luxury of choosing our own work schedule. We were like Uber drivers in that sense.

# SCENE TWO

Belle jumped on me and licked my face to wake me up. The problem was, she was three times heavier than when I got her, so it wasn't as cute anymore. Just to clarify, Belle was my bitch. Like an actual woof-woof, four-legged, covered in fur, dog. A samoyed to be precise — those big white fluffy ones that always look like they're smiling. She had just celebrated her first birthday, but in her mind, she was still a puppy. I wanted to get a boy dog and call him either Alfred, after Alfred the Great — and Batman's butler — or Shakespeare, after, well, Shakespeare, but the breeder only had girls left and I instantly fell in love with her. I toyed around with Lola, Lolly, Dolly, and Mildred, but luckily landed on Belle. I wish I had a better story like the first time I saw her, I could hear church bells in the distance, that her dogmother was Kristen Bell, or even that there was a bell around her collar when I picked her up, but it was completely random. It worked and she seemed to like it.

# THE LOST ROMANTICS

I don't know what compelled me to get a dog—the company, I suppose—but it had completely changed my life. It forced me to get up early every morning, forced me to go for long walks, and gave me a sense of responsibility that I was, perhaps, lacking. We had a Jack Russel growing up, but I didn't remember it being such hard work. The first thing I learned was that a Samoyed probably wasn't the smartest of choices for a single guy living in London, but much to everyone's surprise, I was managing just fine. Sure there were times when I wanted to shoot myself, or her, especially when all my clothes were covered in hair—hair everywhere, so much hair—but then she'd trot over and look at me with those sad eyes and all would be forgiven. Plus, let's be honest, I thought she'd be quite the lady magnet. Most of the people around me had small, tiny-little dogs because they had small, tiny-little apartments, but I lived in a pretty decent sized open-plan pad on the corner of New Cavendish and Marylebone High Street, so every time I took her out for a walk, I felt like a bit of a celebrity. Girls would smile as we passed them on the street and at least one would have to stop to pet her soft, plush coat. They'd ask her name, I'd ask their name, and that's all it took. I wish. A conversation rarely brewed, but it was a nice pick me up in the morning. I tried to do at least one long, leisurely stroll, unless it was raining or I was hungover, in which case it would be a short, brisk lap around the block.

Holly, who lived just on the other side of Baker Street, usually came to pick Belle up around lunchtime. I found her through one of the dog-walking apps, but after only a few bookings, she also absolutely fell in love with her and offered to take her for afternoon jogs around Regent's Park for free. She was great with dogs and was dying for one of her own, but it just wasn't the right time for her. The building her apartment was in didn't allow pets and she planned on moving back home to Iowa after she graduated, so it really was a match made in heaven. So much so that when I had to go away for the weekend, which was quite often, Holly would come over and stay at mine. She was a student at Regent's — where we all went — and was sharing a flat with three other girls, so it was like a mini vacation for her, too.

# SCENE THREE

I always had trouble focusing on, or even starting, work when I knew I had plans in the evening. The problem was, I had plans most evenings, which was why it took me so long to ever finish a painting. I liked knowing that I had nothing else on and nowhere else to be so that I could fully get in the zone. I wondered if other artists were as professional at procrastinating as I was.

I wrote it off as a free day, so decided to call Hugo to see if he wanted to meet for a late lunch or some drinks before the party. He was always my first point of call, even though he was usually too busy. I found that the trick was to get him early, before he went to work, otherwise, he'd fill his day with meetings, and his evening with some sort of random event, activity, or date. I suggested Colbert on Sloane Square, seeing as we'd need to be in the area for the party later that evening anyway, but you'd have thought I'd asked him to go south of the river. Hugo hated going into Chelsea. He found it such a chore, even though he lived ten minutes away, in Mayfair. We all kind of lived in a straight line. Close enough that we were walking distance, but far enough that we didn't share a Waitrose. I was, of course, in Marylebone, Hugo was off Berkeley Square, Will was in Chelski, and Cali, I don't even think the Lord knew where he was half of the time. Keeping up with Cali wasn't easy. I knew he had a flat in Knightsbridge that he stayed in sometimes, his parents had a fuck-off mansion in Hampstead that was empty for most of the year, but if he was with a girl, he'd check in to a hotel. Which hotel depended on the girl and how hard he felt he had to try to impress her. In fact, he'd often refer to his conquests by where he slept with them. We'd all recently heard of the Hilton Park Lane ho, the Four Seasons floozy, and The Dorchester Duchess. It was rather offensive, and a fine example of why I sometimes questioned our friendship, but when you were in his company, he was ever so charming and embarrassingly entertaining. It's no excuse, but that's just who he was.

Anyway, it took some convincing, but Hugo, who was unofficially my best friend, reluctantly agreed to a long, maybe too boozy, lunch.

"Let's go to Harrods, I still need to get Cali a gift," I proposed.

"Sscheisse! I didn't get him anything either."

As we hiked up Sloane Street, Hugo searched for reasons why it wasn't necessary to get him anything at all. "I mean, we're grown men. Surely, it's customary to just buy him a drink." It wasn't clear if he was asking me or telling me.

"It's an open bar," I stated. "Cali always has an open bar at his parties."

"Yeah, but—"

"But nothing," I said, sternly. "It's his birthday, and we're getting him a gift. Not together, because that would be gay, but individually, we're both going to get him something nice and thoughtful." Like all other holidays, birthdays had a set tradition. At Christmas, you had to eat Turkey, even if you prefer a juicier chicken. You had to buy a real tree, even though its needles would sting your feet when you walked around your house. You had to eat mince pies, drink mulled wine, play charades with your drunk grandmother and overly excited uncle, pull Christmas crackers, wear those flimsy toilet paper crowns, and listen to the same Christmas playlist over, and over, and over again. It's just the way things were. At Easter, you had to have a chocolate egg. At weddings, the bride had to have something new, something old, something borrowed, and something blue. Valentine's Day required a teddy bear, a box of chocolates in the shape of a heart, and champagne. It was the same for birthdays. At birthdays, you had to blow out candles, eat cake, and get presents. I was a firm believer that certain traditions, even if created by Hollywood, even if you didn't like them, should be upheld. I wasn't a fan of the modern London birthday party where everyone just got together at a restaurant or a bar, paid for their own dinner, bought their own drinks, and didn't even sing *Happy Birthday*. If you were going to host a party, you should host a party. "Cali's doing his bit, so it's not just our choice, it's our duty to buy him a present and have it wrapped with a bow."

"Fine," Hugo conceded.

I got Cali a crocodile skin card holder from Tom Ford, which was very Cali, Hugo got him a book about gin and a rare bottle that was featured in it, and the gift wrapping elves did the rest. Mission accomplished.

# SCENE FOUR

We still had some time to kill before the party, so we decided to go for some pre-drinks, or should I say, some more pre-drinks.

"Phene?" I put forward.

Hugo gave it some thought and then countered, "The Botanist?"

"But the Phene has Hells. Plus it's Lucy's dad's place, so we'd be supporting a friend."

"But it's six o'clock on a Tuesday, so The Botanist will be busier."

We both knew he meant that there'd be more girls there. "Botanist it is." I loved The Phene, but was already getting a little tired, and a comfy corner in a cosy pub would have been the end of me.

Unfortunately, The Botanist wasn't as buzzing as we'd hoped, but there were still a few familiar faces. Will's neighbour, Mrs Chester, was standing at the bar with her vicious little Miniature Schnauzer, Ruffles, as was the girl from @the_luxury_edit who did those travel and makeup videos on Instagram. Her name escaped me, but she was pretty pretty.

We scanned the room for a seat, and lo and behold, we saw Emma, Hugo's most recent three-monther, having a glass of wine with a girlfriend. It was a common pattern with him. He'd go out with a girl for three months and then find a ridiculous reason why he had to break up with her. I could tell by his fake smile and underacted enthusiasm that he wasn't exactly thrilled to see her. To be honest, she didn't seem too thrilled to see us either. They had a weird relationship. Sometimes, they were inseparable and went on romantic weekend getaways, but most of the time, they were so independent of each other, you'd never know either of them was dating anyone. He didn't understand it either, even though he was the primary instigator. We approached, slowly.

"Emma!" I greeted, and then without much else, "Aren't you going to introduce me to your friend?" Even I could hear the sharkiness in my voice.

"Millie, Max. Max, Millie."

Millie had no makeup on and her hair was tied up in a messy bun, but I was a sucker for a girl in lulullemons, especially when they had those mesh cutouts. As I offered her my hand to get acquainted, Emma quickly downed her glass of wine and got up to leave. She gave Hugo a quick kiss on the cheek and excused, "We're actually running late for a yogalates class at the Chelsea Sports Centre."

They were already halfway out the door before I had a chance to salute, "Hope to see you again soon, Millie."

Hugo broke his silence, "Don't be a creep."

"Am I not even allowed to talk to girls anymore?" Before he could answer, "Fine, we'll just file it as another one that ended before it began." He ignored me, but was thrilled that we got their table. He really hated standing. "So, did you invite her to Cali's party?"

It took him a moment, but then he started rambling, "She doesn't really like Cali. I think she's busy tonight anyway. It's not really her thing. We're not really there yet."

I sat quietly waiting for the real reason. We'd been friends long enough for him to know that I wouldn't give up my silent interrogation that easily.

He finally admitted, "Fine, I'm thinking of breaking up with her."

"Why? Emma's great. She's sweet, she's kind, she's thoughtful, she's pretty, she's... sweet." She might have been a little intimidated by me and didn't trust me enough to go out with one of her friends, but I was still Team Emma. She was good for Hugo. I held my silence to press him further.

"There's nothing wrong with her. She's sweet." Only, when he said it, it sounded like sweet was a beastly quality. Again, "You know, she's sweet."

I may not have agreed with his tone, but I kind of knew what he meant.

He continued, trying harder to justify his reason, "She's not *the one*."

"Ah, *the one*. Well, I guess it's better than her forehead being too big, or that she pronounced the word 'bath' wrong, or that you don't like any of her shoes," which were all reasons he'd broken up with girls in the past. "What does *the one* even mean?" It implied that there was only one person in the whole world that you belonged with, but we all knew that was a load of codswallop. How do you know she's not?"

"You just know," he said, carelessly.

"Will we really ever find the girl that ticks all of our boxes though? Should we even be looking for that girl?" I questioned.

"Probably not."

"Is there an element of settling in settling down?" The more I asked, the more I found myself unsure, so I continued to fight Emma's corner. "You can do a lot worse than Emma. Wait, let me correct myself. You have done a lot worse than Emma."

"You can talk. Why are you still single, Mr My Standards Are So High That I'm Going To Die Alone?"

"Low blow." Making sure the conversation didn't continue down that path, and fully conscious that I was starting to sound like a Jewish grandmother, I asked, "Why wouldn't you marry Emma?"

He flip-flopped around, "She's nice, but she's a little boring. She's a little normal. She's a little plain. Is basic the right word?"

I shrugged my shoulders, but, again, I kind of knew what he meant. I felt there was more to it though.

"She's not…" To clarify his point, he pulled out his phone and opened Instagram. Without having to scroll too far down his feed, he showed me the latest posts from @lararunarsson, @madtev, @natalee.007, @khloe… Surprised, I made him scroll back up a few, "Wait, are you following Khloe Kardashian?"

"No!" he roared, as he clicked into the profile. "Who do you think I am? It's a different Khloe." He picked his favourite pics and showed them off like he was a proud grandmother.

His app navigation was slick, precise, and well versed. I nodded my approval, so he went back to his feed. @tiffanytothxoxo, @indithew_, and my personal favourite, @katrinakbowden. "Stunning, each and every one of them, but you do realise they're not real. They only exist in your phone."

He didn't seem convinced, so continued scrolling. "And they're cool. They're always doing fun stuff. Even when they go to Starbucks, it's like a thing."

Peeking over to make sure I didn't miss any, I half-heartedly continued, "They don't look like that in real life. It's just a combination of makeup, lighting, Facetune 2, and careful curation of hundreds of photos." It sounded like I was trying to convince myself. I forced myself to sit back. "But seriously — "

Hugo offered his rebuttal simply by looking up from his phone and giving a smiling nod to the immaculate Instagram influencer that was still standing by the bar.

"Touché."

We were so caught up in Instaworld, we had completely missed the two girls that had taken the table next to us. When I looked up, they giggled. It was clear that they had enjoyed our conversation because one of them added, "It's not bad, it's just different now." It was either a very intelligent and well thought out remark, or utter gibberish. I had already lost the wind from my argument, so agreed with her exchange.

We paid the bill, and as we were leaving, one of them grabbed Hugo's phone and started scanning her Snapchat ghost code thingy. I don't know what surprised me more; the fact that she was so forward for an English girl that wasn't in a Richard Curtis movie, the fact that she gave him her Snapchat, or that Hugo still had Snapchat installed on his phone. He played it cool, as if it happened to him on the daily, and bopped out.

"Snapchat? Really?" I bellowed.

"I know you are still asking girls for their addresses so that you can send them a handwritten letter…" he mocked, "but you heard her, it's the new normal."

"I thought Snapchat was for kids in secondary school to send dirty pictures to each other."

He corrected me, "You don't have to be in secondary school to do that," and then teased, "but I wouldn't worry about it, she didn't try to add you."

"Bastard!"

# SCENE FIVE

Hugo was ready for another drink and to get the evening going, but I insisted that we grab a bite to eat first. I always had to insist that we eat. I'd learned my lesson the hard way one too many times. As we walked up King's Road, I, a pseudo-Luddite, continued my rant about how apps like Snapchat, and all social media for that matter, had ruined life as we knew it. Again, very annoyingly, Hugo repeated the girl's words, "It's not bad, it's just different." He was in an abnormally cocky mood and began his rant, "Sure, things have changed, but change isn't always a bad thing. In fact, change is usually a good thing. If it wasn't for change, we'd still be shitting outside."

I couldn't argue with that.

He went on, "We as a society are so scared of change or anything different that we automatically label change as bad."

I wasn't prepared to lose another argument, so retaliated, "But we spend so much of our day looking at screens, we're losing our ability to communicate with each other outside of the digital world. We're forgetting how to talk to people, and how to treat people." It was getting heated, and I wasn't backing down. "Kids as young as three years old are glued to their iPads, consuming a constant cascade of crap. When we were young, and I get the irony or whatever it is of me saying that, we used to go out and make friends. We used to climb trees in the park, play conkers, swap football cards, skateboard down hills, scrape our knees, and play with ants and worms."

"Different, but not necessarily bad," he repeated smugly.

I couldn't understand why he refused to agree with me. Surely, the whole world agreed with me.

It was an intense game of verbal tennis, and when it was his turn, he served, "Maybe, in the future, the skills that you think are so important just won't matter anymore. Maybe, if the world is going more digital, it is important that the three-year-old knows how to code. Maybe they don't need to know how to climb trees. I mean, we aren't apes anymore. Maybe we're just evolving.

"Interesting, but keep your FIRE ALARM ethics to yourself." It was obvious I was clutching. I needed backup. We were passing Will's street, so I suggested we see if he wanted to join us for dinner before the party. We were both under strict instructions not to feel free to pop in whenever we were in the neighbourhood, but the lager in me was willing to deal with Will's wrath.

# WILL

Those two drunk morons were always bickering about one thing or another. I often wondered how they were such good friends because they hardly ever seemed to see eye to eye on anything. Maybe it was just habitual. Oddly, I agreed with Max that people spent too much time on their phones. It was a sign of a weakening society. I could have intervened and put them out of their misery, but if I'd learned anything, it was to let them sort it out for themselves and not to get involved.

"Let's have another drink first," Hugo proposed. "Will's got some catching up to do."

"He can have a beer at Five Guys," Max decided.

Hugo looked disgusted. "I thought we were going to Byron."

A tall, slim blonde strutted past, bringing them both to a halt. She knew they were looking, most likely because they didn't try to hide it in any way. At least they agreed on one thing. Personally, I wasn't that interested. "Too much makeup," I commented, out of character.

"What are you talking about? She was a perfect ten," Max argued.

"It was all hair and makeup."

Hugo backed him up, "Okay, but with that, she was hot."

"I prefer the natural look," I stated, wondering why I was getting into it.

"So do I, but she should be able to pull off both. The natural look is good for cuddling, but sometimes you need her to look like that," Max said incoherently. He was still trying to sneak a final peek.

Hugo settled back down a little faster, "In the future, they probably won't even have makeup. It's quite a primitive concept if you think about it. Women painting their faces to attract men, or feel more confident," he presented.

He had a point.

He continued, "People a hundred years from now will look at our generation and laugh at us."

There was no surprise that Max weighed in, "True, but I still like it in this generation. Our ideas of beauty have already been formed. It's too late for us now. It's up to us to teach the next generation to not find flawless skin, smoky bedroom eyes, luscious red lips, cute rosy cheeks..." he drifted off into his own fantasy world.

I agreed with Hugo, but I didn't think he was right, "The big cosmetic conglomerates are too powerful to let that happen."

"I do like a red lip," Hugo confessed.

"Especially when they..." Max affirmed, which initiated them both to high five like a couple of adolescent American teenagers.

I was already monstrously regretting my decision of opening the door and agreeing to join them. I could have had the leftover noodles in my fridge, read my magazine, shown my face at the party for a few minutes, and been back in bed before midnight. C'est la vie. Seeing as I was out-out, it was time to put my foot down. I did a quick Google search in my head of where we were and what suitable eating establishments were within walking distance. I'd usually go to Ziani's or Polpo, but needed something slightly less off-piste to veer them off the scent of junk. There was The Ivy, but I knew Made in Italy would be less of a fight. Another thing I had learnt was that it was best not to ask, so I let them continue squabbling. Lead and they shall follow. It was cute that they thought they were getting burgers, but we'd already been seated and brought a round of Morettis before they realised where we were. Like I said, morons.

They caught me up on the day's events. The first point went to Hugo. I got Cali a sweet little card that read, *'Happy Anniversary of Your Birth,'* but no gift. On Hugo breaking up with Emma, I had to go with Max again, but for a slightly different reason. She was sweet. "What is it this time; she likes to call you Daddy while you're having sex and you find it weird, or is she just too loud in bed?" They really did bring out the worst in me.

Max spoke first, "You have met Emma, right?"

"It's always the quiet ones," I joked.

"Evidently so. You're supposed to be the gentleman one of the group. Even I didn't ask that," Max chimed.

"Actually, I'm simply reciting some of the previous reasons."

Hugo finally spoke up, "None of those reasons, unfortunately. I don't really have a reason."

Max pulled out his phone and showed me a short video of a girl in her car, drinking a Starbucks iced coffee, talking about Lord knows what.

I didn't understand.

"That's the reason," Max explained.

"Who is she?" I asked, genuinely curious.

Hugo rolled his eyes, but Max was on a mission, "Some girl in California. No one we know, but an idea he's in love with. Go, Will."

I took a small sip of my beer, and proceeded to offer them both some advice, "Have I ever told you guys what morons you are?"

"Me?" Max exclaimed.

In my opinion, he was just as guilty, "Yes. What you guys are doing isn't healthy. If you continue with this moronic behaviour, you'll never be happy because you'll always be looking for something better."

"That's exactly what I was trying to tell him," Max said, trying to side with me.

I didn't want to sound rude, but had to be honest with him, "You're just as bad, if not worse. At least Hugo gives them a chance and goes out with them for three months. If you're not careful, you're going to end up that creepy old guy chasing 19-year-old girls at Tiger Tiger"

Hugo put his arm around Max, "Don't worry, mate. Luckily, girls like older guys."

And that's why they were such good friends. "Morons."

Two giant metre-long pizzas arrived as I steered the conversation to something more benign before it got too hostile. To be fair, I was single too, but it wasn't because I was too picky or in love with an Instamodel, it was because the right girl just hadn't come along. I believed that you shouldn't go out looking for love; you should just focus on living your best life. If someone naturally entered it, that was great, and if they didn't, then that was fine, too. Just then, I was brought to a pause, frozen mid-slice by a ravishing young lady on a table in the back who had just gotten up to leave. Long black wavy hair, tanned skin, big bright eyes, and the cutest dimples when she smiled to thank the waiter for handing her her coat. She was with a few other friends, all dressed to the nines, and the way she moved was a definite ten. Mental note, research the origin of the idiom, *to the nines*.

The guys noticed I wasn't paying attention anymore. Hugo didn't make it too obvious, but as she walked past,

Max embarrassingly asked for confirmation, "Red dress?" He knew my type.

She must have heard because she looked back and gifted us a smile. There was a moment of silence on our table. It was like an angel had flown by.

I had to say, "You're an idiot, Max!"

"Well, at least she gave you a smile. If I hadn't of said anything..."

Stuffed, unable to even look at another slice, our postprandial palaver somehow reverted back to dating.

"Twenty-six is the perfect age," Max opened with. "They've gone through university, found themselves through travelling, kissed enough frogs never to look back with regret, but still have that innocence of youth."

"And they're still flexible, taut, perky," Hugo added, cheekily.

I was still thinking about the girl in the red dress, holding on to her rich, caramel scent in the air.

"How old is Emma?" Max enquired.

Hugo breathed out, almost with disappointment, "Thirty-one."

Surprised, I rejoined the conversation. "Wow, she doesn't look it. I would have guessed around twenty-five."

"Thanks, I'll tell her you said that, but after thirty, girls start getting the desperate itch to settle down, get married, have kids…" Hugo replied, immediately unsure whether what he had just said was okay or not.

I wasn't sure either. As a generalisation? Maybe. For good reason? Perhaps. I wouldn't have phrased it as desperation, personally. I considered his statement and how to correct it, but Max softened it by adding, "It's not just women, I'm ready for the whole marriage, 2.5 kids, white picket fence, golden retriever…"

"Yeah?" Even I wasn't sure about some of those concepts, and I was clearly more mature and settled than him.

"I'm ready. Got the venue picked out for the wedding, mulled over the menu, the playlist, the honeymoon. I even have the perfect engagement ring picked out."

"All you're missing is the girl," I teased. "What does the ring look like?"

"It's from Graff." You could see the excitement on his face. He put down his beer and pulled out his phone to show me a picture he had saved on his camera roll. "It's the Paragon round brilliant cut series. Simple platinum band. Very elegant, very —"

"Three single grown men on a night out and we're seriously talking about the cut of the dress you're going to wear on your wedding day?" Hugo interjected, with slight annoyance.

I had to point out, "You're not single."

"Chelsea won," Max coughed, in a lame attempt to redeem himself.

Hugo called over the waiter and asked for the bill.

# SCENE SEVEN

Luckily, the party wasn't far, otherwise, I would have had to endure yet another useless, never-ending debate whether it was okay for guys to talk about weddings and the sort. Don't get me wrong, I had an opinion on the matter, but when it came to those two, serious discussions usually took a risqué turn after one of them would make a silly comment that sat uncomfortably on the fence of political correctness.

Cali had hired out Raffles, so it was a quick hundred yard dash up King's Road. Apart from Annabel's, which was completely different, Raffles was probably the only other club left in London that I didn't mind going to. I was expecting twenty, maybe twenty-five people, but should have known better. As we approached, it was busier than I'd ever seen it. Even busier than a Saturday night when the queue alone was thirty strong. All familiar faces, but only a few that I actually knew.

The same lady you always saw at the door of every club, with her sharp cheekbones, vivid red lipstick, tightly pulled back ponytail, and long black trench coat resting on her shoulders checked for our names on her clipboard. Max and I were given the green light to proceed past the red velvet barrier, but Hugo didn't seem to be on the list.

"You've seen me here a thousand times," he pleaded while pulling out his phone to call Cali. "He's obviously purposely trying to make our lives difficult. You know I know him." The lady seemed unfazed and continued to welcome those who were on the list. Failing to get a hold of Cali, Hugo started panicking, even though he knew for certain it was a wind-up. "Come. On. You're seriously not going to let me in? I think I'm even a member. Don't you have to let members in?"

"I'm so sorry, it's a private event tonight," she replied, coldly.

"Have a good night, Hugs," Max yelled, as he pretended to hop in.

The music was already blaring, so it took a little extra effort for me to assure him, "We'll go in and find Cali. Just wait here."

"Yeah, we'll definitely be back," Max sarcastically teased.

The lady overheard our theatrics and then revealed, "I do have a Mr Fire Alarm on the list, in case that's you."

With a great big roll of his eyes, Hugo pushed past and unclipped the rope to let himself in. Under his breath, he complained, "It's not even funny," but Max and the lady with the clipboard shared a good chuckle.

A new song started playing, perfectly synced to our entrance. I had no idea what it was, but Max had his arms up and seemed to know every word, "Dance for me, dance for me, dance for me, oh, oh, oh!" We obliged and shimmied our way through the crowd to Cali's usual table, where a waitress had already been instructed to pour us champagne. He only ever ordered Dom, so I was sold.

"Hugo! They let you in?" Cali squeaked.

Hugo replied with a middle finger and then went in for a hug.

We toasted the birthday boy and then settled in around the table to speak to some of the other guests. I don't know how or where he found them, but Cali was always surrounded by a gaggle of gorgeous gals. Max was like a kid in a candy store, shooting the few Russian words he kept in his arsenal. Hugo was immediately engrossed in the drinks menu, so I scanned the room for others we might know, or would want to say hello to. Cali knew a lot of important and influential people, or at least their kids, so it was a good opportunity to network.

I followed the smoky beams of colour that danced around the room, settling on a table two away. There she was. The girl in the red dress from the restaurant. Time slowed down. Her long, shiny hair held in the air a beat longer, as she bounced and swayed like a Jaguar; majestic, dangerous, and full of grace. Again, I found myself frozen in complete awe. Locked into the moment, I pictured our first date at Quaglino's. I saw us cuddled up on my sofa, reading. I saw us on holiday together, hiking, cycling, and walking hand in hand on the beach. My train of thought only crashed when Max put his arm around me. The music returned to full volume with a shockwave, as if I had just come up from underwater.

"I think I'm in love with the Latvian girl in the purple dress on our table," Max yelled.

I quickly glanced over my shoulder as a formality and then turned right back, not wanting to lose track of my own new love.

"Oh, look! It's your girl from the restaurant." His point turned into a wave.

I could feel my cheeks burning red.

She laughed, waved back, and then continued cavorting with her friends.

"He who hesitates, masturbates," Max rapped before swinging back to his girl.

I knew I had to go over and talk to her, but the music was too loud. There were too many other people. What does one even say in that situation? For the next hour, I tried relentlessly to make eye contact, open up our circle, and up the cheer on our table in order to catch her attention, but nothing worked and I eventually lost sight of her. By that point, Cali and Hugo were rolling dice and playing cricket on the dance floor, Max was in deep conversation with a girl that wasn't the Latvian in the purple dress, and I, I sat alone, kicking myself for not taking the advice I would have dished out of going up to her and introducing myself while I had the chance.

I was contemplating calling it a night when I felt a tap on my shoulder. It was her, holding one of the Jeroboams of Grey Goose from our table.

"Mind if I steal this?" she asked, playfully.

"Sure. Be my guest. Of course!" I knew I had to say something, but none of the words I had been juggling in my head all night came to mind.

She was struggling with the size of the bottle, and before I had a chance to be a gentleman, she asked, "Can you help me?"

I sprung out of my seat and grabbed it from her. She picked up two glasses, used them to scoop up some ice, and held them out. I gently poured, making sure not to spill any. She held them up in the air, surprised at how healthy my measures were. I buried the bottle back into the bucket and picked up a couple of mixers. "Orange or Cranberry?"

"Tonic."

I frantically searched our table and the table behind us. "I can go and get some from the bar. Just wait right here —"

"Cranberry is fine," she giggled.

I topped them up with what was only a splash of juice. "I'm better at making Ribena, I promise."

She handed me one of the drinks and placed a straw in each. She took a sip and winced, "Just how I like my Ribena."

"Strong —" quickly upgrading my comment to, "With a lot of vodka?"

She laughed and put her hand on my arm.

"I'm William," I said, extending my hand for a handshake. A handshake! Really?

"Nice to meet you, William," she said in a faux English accent.

"Are you making fun of me?"

Again, attempting and failing to sound like BoJo, "Of course not, I wouldn't do such a thing."

"Well, where are you from?"

"France."

"I gathered as much. I meant, where in France?"

"Paris," she responded quickly, proudly returning to her mother accent.

"Bless you." She didn't get it, so I teased further, "I thought there was an 's' at the end of Paris, and I sure don't remember there being a throat scratchy growl in the middle."

She laughed and held her glass close to her chest. Fiddling with her straw as she dared to take another sip, she teased me right back with her big brown eyes. Even in the darkness of the club, I could see all of her. We stood there staring and smiling at each other uncontrollably. Words were not necessary. Before I could assess whether it was appropriate to go in for a kiss, her friend came up behind her and started to pull her away. I couldn't let her leave, so I pulled her back, shouting in her ear, "I don't even know your name."

She leant in and aggressively pressed her lips against mine before being dragged off by her evil witch of a bitch. Just like that, she vanished into the crowd, leaving me standing there, clinging onto the moment.

# SCENE EIGHT

After every big night out, we'd always meet up the next morning to debrief. You could say it was another one of our traditions. Cali called it the Billionaire Breakfast Club, which was grossly inaccurate as none of us were billionaires, and we usually met at a hotel in Central London rather than a yacht in the South of France. As always, Claridge's was packed. As always, Max was the first to arrive so had gotten us a table. And, as always, Cali, who was staying at the hotel, was late. He literally had no excuse, so we didn't bother waiting for him. We covered the table with our plates of fruit, cold cuts, cheeses, and pastries. I added an omelette and a pot of green tea, Hugo went for porridge and coffee, and Max did his usual eggs Benedict with a glass of each of their juice options because he could never decide which he was in the mood for. To say we were creatures of habit would have been an understatement. We would have been very easy to poison. Cali finally traipsed in and plopped himself down, animating his hangover with every movement.

"Fuck me, that's a nice watch!" Max cursed as he took hold of Cali's wrist. "AP?"

Cali straightened up with pride, "Audemars Piguet Royal Oak Offshore Tourbillon Chronograph. It's the 45mm. It's about time you noticed. I was wearing it last night."

When Max finally let go of his arm, it made a pitstop at one of Hugo's plates. I think Cali did it on purpose because he knew how annoyed and uncomfortable Hugo got when people picked food off his plate.

"A two-hundred-thousand-pound watch and he's still too cheap to pay for his own buffet," Hugo moaned, defeatedly.

"Two fifty. It was a present to myself. You only turn thirty-two once."

I had to admit, it was a pretty nice watch, but I wasn't going to give Cali the pleasure that easily, "APs are for RAVs —Russians, Arabs, and villains."

"No, the GS elevator guy was talking about Richard Mille. This is next level shit. You wouldn't understand."

I didn't agree, but I did understand. We all had pretty nice timepieces. Max wore a Panerai, I was building my collection of IWCs, and Hugo, well, Hugo fashioned an Apple Watch, but he had a really nice Patek in his safe. "Aren't you worried you'll scratch it, or lose it, or someone will chop off your hand for it?"

"I'm not going to wear it every day? Plus, it's insured for even more."

As we were talking about it, a heavyset Arab man approached our table on his way out of the restaurant. At first, I assumed it was one of Cali's uncles or something. "Nice watch."

"Thanks!"

"Can I see it?"

Without any hesitation, Cali unbuckled it and handed it over to the stranger. Sure, he looked like the kind of fellow who belonged to an actual billionaire breakfast club, but I was on high alert.

The man inspected it closely. "Yallah, I'll give you three."

I looked at Cali wide-eyed.

"Thanks, but I just got it, so I think I'm going to hold on to it." Cali put his hand out for it back before the man got too comfortable with it.

As he was walking off, he said, "If you change your mind, let me know. I'll be here till Friday."

"You idiot Cali, you could have just made fifty grand," Max said while buttering a piece of toast.

"Yeah, you could have used it to buy your own buffet instead of stealing off my plate," Hugo added

He took that as an invitation to help himself to another slice of cheese. "So, Max said you're breaking up with Emily."

"It's Emma," Hugo corrected. "And if Max continues spreading gossip, he's going to end up on The Real Housewives of Marylebone Village."

"Out of date reference, old friend," Max defended.

I made my position clear, "I told him to stop being a moron."

"Why are we talking about this?" Hugo asked. "I know, I know, she's sweet. I should settle down with her—"

"Au contraire, mon frère. I'm on your side. You're too young to settle down. There are too many hot chicas out there. I say dump the boring bitch."

"Why, so he can end up like you, having meaningless no-strings sex with a different beautiful woman every night?" It was unclear if Max's question sided him with me, or if it was supposed to be sarcastic. I think his position might have changed as he asked it because there was an air of bitterness or jealousy humoured in.

"Sometimes it's two," Cali bragged. "All I'm saying is that we men aren't designed to be monogamous creatures. It's not natural. Relationships are so overrated. Why waste all that time and energy on the same girl?"

I knew Cali was seasoning his words to get a rise out of me, but it was working. "A crazy little thing called love," I sang.

"Love is just a made-up concept you've been brainwashed to believe, Will. You'll eventually lose interest and stop doing the things she likes, and then she'll stop doing the things you like. Why put yourself through all the heartache, the cheating, lying, fighting?" he said, passionately. In fact, it was the most passionate and involved I'd ever seen him in one of our conversations, but I knew I was right.

"When you meet someone and fall in love, you'll know what I'm talking about."

"I love a different girl every week. I have a lot of love to share," he joked. "For every hot girl out there, or in Hugo's case, sweet girl, there's a guy that's tired of fucking her."

"Charming. How is it that you don't get slapped more?" I asked, genuinely wondering.

"Girls like it when you talk to them a little rough. It shows them you're a man. It shows them who's boss," Cali responded while signalling Hugo to pass him the butter. Instead, Hugo signalled a waiter.

"Treat them mean, keep them keen. It's a psychological fact. It reminds them of their daddy or something. They appreciate cutting through all the bullshit and just saying things the way they are."

Holding back my outrage, "I don't think you know the meaning of the word fact."

Cali pulled out his room key. "The evidence is lying in my bed upstairs right now. Room 208. Go up and check. If you're lucky, and not too nice to her, she might even give you a morning blowy. Lord knows you need it"

Croissant in hand, Max woke up, "Can I go up and check?"

"You guys are exactly what's wrong with the world today. Scared little boys afraid of commitment, afraid of getting hurt." I said with vigour.

Hugo saw how heated I was getting, so came to my aid, "I'm with Will here. You can still be a nice guy. That's the only way you'll find a nice girl. They're becoming wise to that whole cool, broken, bad boy that needs saving act. It works when you're in your twenties, but now it's just more work than it's worth.""

Max was distant, smiling over Cali's shoulder. The waiter approached our table. "Good morning, Mr Cali. Can I get you gentlemen anything?"

Max pointed in the direction he was looking, "I want that."

We all looked over, expecting to see a young, pretty blonde, but I was pleasantly surprised to see the cutest old couple sitting next to each other on the same side of the table. The old chap was pouring the love of his life a cup of tea, as she sorted through a newspaper, dividing the sections between them. A routine they had surely practised over many years.

"More tea? A newspaper?" the waiter asked.

Cali excused the clueless server, "No, nothing, thanks."

"I think that's what Will is talking about," Max said. He was right. The display couldn't have been a better example. "That's happiness."

"I put the penis in happiness," Cali vulgared.

"Uncouth," was all I had left to say. I don't know how I could have made it clearer. He was too much for me sometimes.

"Talking of putting penises in things, rumour has it, you were getting on pretty well with a girl last night, Willie."

I hated it when Cali called me that. I looked at Hugo and Max to see who the source was. Max.

"Well, did you sleep with her?"

"No, but it wasn't just about sleeping with her. You do realise that sex is not the ultimate goal, right?"

"The whole world revolves around sex. It's much more powerful than love, or even money. At the end of the day, no matter how much you deny it, it's all about sex," Cali articulated. "Sex is the only reason we do anything. We're all animals. Presidents, CEOs, the poor waiter that works like a donkey; it's all so that they can get better, more frequent sex. We live for sex. The only difference is, I'm not ashamed to admit it."

I had become tired of the conversation, so to end it, I forfeited, "Call me old fashioned, but I still look for companionship, respect, a life partner to grow old with, like those two," I nodded to the old couple who were now holding hands. "Each to their own. You do you"

"So who's this mystery girl you got on so well with then?" Cali asked, softer, to show that we were still friends.

"Stunning. Fiery. Good kisser," I gloated to show that I wasn't a complete bore.

Cali patted me on the shoulder to congratulate me, "You dog. What was her name?"

"That's the problem, I didn't get her name or number."

He patted again, "Well, what did she look like? I can give you her number if you want."

"And how would you do that?"

Hugo butted in, "You know, for the smart one of the group, you're not terribly smart sometimes. It was his party. His guest list. He invited everyone there."

A rush of elation ran through me, but quickly left when I realised it would be wrong. "If she wanted to give me her number, she would have given it to me."

"Will, the forever alone gentleman." Cali teased. "Big tits?"

"No! I mean, yes, they were pretty nice. Who even asks that? Who even notices that?"

"I do," Cali said.

Max, still eating, thought he'd help out. "She had more than a handful, but she was more of a butt girl, I'd say. Tight red dress that fit her like a glove. Red lips with red soles to match."

I didn't feel comfortable with the direction we were going in, so I steered it back, "Silky black hair, short, kind of Latina looking, but she was French. From Paris."

"Zara," Cali muttered.

"Yeah, she kind of looked like a Zara," I agreed. I was excited that I at least had a name for my dream girl.

"Those French girls are dirty," Max added, trying to take the tone right back down.

"Didn't you live in Paris for a bit, Cali?" Hugo asked.

"Yes. I did." He stood up and threw his napkin on the table with unannounced anger. "With my sister, Zara!"

Shit! Cali stormed off. I felt like I should have apologised, but I hadn't done anything wrong. Maybe one of us should have gone after him, but we all just sat there in silence, awkwardly looking at each other instead.

"I say, Will. You shouldn't have felt up Cali's sister like that," Max blurted.

"I didn't. You were the one talking about her arse."

"That's pretty low, Will," Max continued, trying to stir things and simultaneously take the blame off of himself.

"Why didn't either of you morons tell me that was Cali's sister?"

"I didn't know. I thought his sister was like ten years old," Hugo defended.

"Yeah, me neither," said Max.

"The way he talks about women, I forgot he even had a sister. You'd think he'd have more respect." I found myself trying to alleviate some of the blame, too.

With a big sigh, Max changed the subject. "Hugo, are we still on for squash today?"

"Yeah, but I forgot my racquet at home and I'm stuck in interviews all morning."

"Just give me your keys and I'll pick it up.

Hugo didn't seem too comfortable with the idea.

"Fancy joining, Will?" Max offered.

"No. Unlike you clowns, I have an actual job to get to. Plus, I need to figure out what to do about this whole Zara situation." I was still in shock, but it seemed like they had moved on.

"Who's Zara," Max asked.

I knew he was being silly, so I got up to leave. "Thanks for breakfast, gentlemen."

# HUGO

Max and I were very close and had been through a lot. We'd shared many an intimate moment, not in a gay way or anything, but we practically lived together during uni, so there wasn't much we didn't know about each other. He knew all of my dirtiest, darkest secrets. Yet, a part of me still felt a little uncomfortable with him being in my house when I wasn't there. He'd asked twice, and I couldn't think of a reasonable reason why not to, so I told him to call me when he got to my place, and I'd buzz him in. One of our first contracts at VIRALARM was working with Amazon on keyless entry systems and security surrounding connected smart home devices, so I had Hay's Mews decked out with all the latest tech. As soon as Max got within twenty feet of my house, I was able to track him on video from my Ring cameras. Even inside the house, I could switch between Alexas to make sure he wasn't doing anything unsavoury. In fact, I still had him as a friend on the *Find My* app on my iPhone, so, technically, I could track his movements all morning. Will, on the other hand, was barely connected to the Internet for that very reason.

It was poor timing when he called because I was just stepping into my office for the third interview of the day. I told him where everything I needed was, and to meet me at my office at noon.

"Just one more thing..." Max said over the phone. "Where do you keep your lotion and paper towels? I might want to relieve some stress before our game."

"Get the fuck out of my house or I'll tell Alexa to start recording and put that shit on PornHub." I hung up as fast as I could, but realised that I was already in earshot of my next candidate. "I'm so sorry. I have a friend in my house being childish," I explained. At the sound of a cute giggle, I looked up from my phone to see a petite redhead waiting across my desk. She was sitting with her knees together, back straight, clutching onto a piece of A4 paper with both hands. Very different from the other two guys I had seen earlier that morning. My first thought was whether she was a natural redhead and if everything matched. My second thought was whether all grown men still thought like pubescent teenagers and were as perverted as I was. Using my friends as a sample, I felt a little better. Cali and Max were a lot worse because they vocalised their deviances, and Will, well, Will was surely an anomaly.

I put my phone down and gave her my full attention, but I had totally gone blank and forgotten what I was supposed to say.

She interrupted the awkward silence and handed me the piece of paper she had been holding on to so tightly that it had creased a little. "I printed off my CV."

"Thanks, Emma? I have a... friend called Emma."

She looked at me, a little confused. "Okay?"

I knew in that moment that it was probably over for sweet, sweet Emma and I, but it was definitely not the right time to think about it. I had to recover the interaction with the Emma that sat in front of me. I put her CV face down on my desk and looked at my screen. "Yes, Emma Crawford. I've got it all here. You see, we're completely paperless here at VIRALARM. We don't have a single printer on our whole floor." Even I found it a little righteous, pretentious, and preachy, but I was proud of the fact.

"Sorry," she spoke, timidly.

"No, I'm sorry," for being an arsehole, I thought. "Why don't you walk me through your experience and why you think you would be a good fit at VIRALARM."

Apart from the rocky start, the rest of the interview went extremely well. She wasn't the most qualified candidate I had seen, but I wasn't hiring a software engineer. I was looking for an Executive Assistant so I could afford to take on someone a little less experienced.

A knock on my door prompted me to check the time. It was one minute past noon. Without waiting for a response, Max paraded into my office as if it were his own. I stood up to officially end the interview and offered her my hand, "Emma, it was really so lovely to meet you. Thanks for coming in. We'll definitely be in touch." I don't think I could have sounded more like a corporate robot if I tried, but I needed to get her out of my office before Max started a conversation with her.

"Emma?" Max fished. "That's Hugo's next exes name."

Too late. He had the biggest mouth sometimes. She gave us both a nervous smile and walked out.

"I'm Max. Nice to meet you, Emma. Hopefully, see you again soon," he yelled after her.

Making sure Emma had left, I turned to Max, "You can be a real dick sometimes, you know that? What did I tell you about creeping?"

"What did I do? I was polite." He helped himself to a bottle of water from the fridge in my office. "She's interviewing to be your EA, so it's better she gets to know how things really work around here. If it was an important meeting, you know I would have waited quietly outside."

That was true. His judgement was sound. He knew when he could be a little cheeky and when to stay quiet, unlike Cali, who didn't extend professional courtesy to anyone. In his eyes, everyone was beneath him, so he said and did whatever he wanted to whomever he wanted because there were rarely any consequences. I secretly admired their confidence and appreciated all the perks it got us when we were out.

"She's cute. You should hire her. Are you going to hire her? Either way, can I call dibs?" Max asked like an excited little schoolboy.

Making sure no one else could hear, "She was really good. And she is pretty hot, but that might be the problem."

Max handed me my squash bag. "Come on, if we get there early and no one else is on the court, we might be able to get a few extra minutes in for free."

My office was on Pall Mall, so it was only a short walk up Haymarket to the squash courts in the Le Méridien on Piccadilly.

"So, why is it a problem if she's hot?" asked Max. "Surely, it's a good thing for business, right? Walking into an important meeting with a hot assistant where all the CEOs are most likely to be men helps."

"Yes, but that's so wrong."

"I agree, but that's the way things are. You're not going to change people's opinions by hiring an ugly assistant. In fact, if you think about it, not hiring her because she's good looking is just as bad. It's reverse affirmative action."

"Reverse affirmative action?" Something gave me the impression that Max's deep concern wasn't so much about equal rights for good looking girls as it was for getting Emma's number. "And that's another thing. Her name's Emma and it would be weird."

"Now you're discriminating against her name?" He was making fair points.

"It will get too confusing. That's why in books and TV shows they never have two characters with the same name." As soon as I said that, I could see him trying his best to think of an example to debunk it.

When he couldn't, he continued, "All I'm saying is that you shouldn't not hire her because she's hot. And either way, you should hook a brotha up."

"Too risky, mate. Hashtag me too, and all that stuff. Don't want to Weinstein it. Oh, and no." The more I verbalised reasons not to hire her, the more I started accepting that she had already gotten the job. Still, for argument's sake, I continued deliberating with Max. "I watched this programme the other day that got me thinking. We've both done things in the past with girls that would be considered a little sketchy today. Freaked me out a bit."

"Speak for yourself. Not me, your honour," he pleaded.

"All those girls you kissed in the clubs without their explicit consent, all those one night stands you had with girls that had been drinking, all those times you had to convince your girlfriend of the time to get a little frisky even if she wasn't in the mood, all those women you've given special treatment to because you thought they were hot…"

A little taken aback, Max thought out loud, "I never, well, there was that one time. And that's not really harassment, is it? Yeah, but technically..."

"Like it or not, you're a bastard. You are a part of the problem." The harshness of my words lightened the tone, but I was only half-joking.

"I thought we were in this together. Different times," he excused.

"Really? That's your defence? I don't think that will hold up in court." I didn't have anything better, but I was glad that we were at least talking about it. It really was the least we could do. I confessed, "Earlier, when I told you to fuck off or I'd put your video on PornHub, Emma, candidate Emma, heard. Lewd comments and inappropriate sexual references like that in the workplace aren't okay."

"That's totally unacceptable," Max said, unsure himself if he was being sarcastic. "Which reminds me, you said PornHub. Is that what you're using these days?"

"No, it's just one of the more popular ones. I said it for comedic effect. YouPorn could have also worked."

"What are you watching these days?" was the exact question I was afraid he'd follow with.

Like I said, we talked about anything and everything, but some things started to feel a little more uncomfortable now that we were older. Saved by the guy at the counter at Le Méridien... or so I thought.

"Because you know it's all about XVideos, right?" Max dropped.

I stayed silent out of embarrassment, but the guy checking us into our courts laughed and nodded in agreement.

When we were clear, I told Max off, "You see, you can't be saying stuff like that. You're spending too much time with Cali. You're becoming a liability. If that were a woman —"

"First, he was the one being rude because he shouldn't have been listening in on our conversation. Second, he loved it. Third, what if he identified as a woman. You shouldn't be so sexist, Hugo."

"Shut up and serve," I said, hoping the conversation would end there. Fearing I sounded too mean, I disclosed, "PornHD."

"Isn't it weird to think that our parents had to use postcards with pin-up girls to get off?"

"Yes, it is a weird thing to think about that." I gave it some thought and was happy with how I worded my response.

Max was far from done. "As much as I disagree with everything Cali says, and I just want to make it clear for the record that I'm not siding with him on this, but in a way, I think a lot of what he was saying at breakfast that it all comes down to sex is true."

"Bastard! That should have been my point," I shouted, already out of breath after the first decent rally.

"We all do it. We're all obsessed with it. We're all here because of it. Isn't it strange that we still don't really talk about it openly."

"That might have been true in the 1950s, but it's everywhere you look these days," I said in between driving the ball along the left side as hard as I could. "You obviously can't stop talking about it."

"Yeah, but I mean we all look down on porn stars, but maybe they've cracked it. They might not know it, but in a way, they've broken through the taboo barrier and are making money from doing something we all love."

"I don't think they've cracked it. They're probably only spreading their crack to buy crack," I cracked.

"Not the girls these days. Not Mia Malkova or Riley Reid," Max proclaimed with victory, as he hit a sneaky cross-court drop shot to win the point.

"Well, if the art thing doesn't work out, you can go and be a male porn star."

"I would, but you closed-minded cocks would slut-shame me."

I was annoyed that he was winning again, and a little concerned with how unfit I was.

He continued, "In a way, it is art. We're the first generation to really have had access to hardcore porn. There must be some sort of psychological effects we're not aware of yet. I mean, I know I'm addicted."

"Stop talking. I know your tactics."

After a few points in silence, he still won the first game and gave me the biggest shit-eating grin. Bastard!

# SCENE TEN

Squash with Max was exhausting, both physically and mentally. I felt emotionally drained. The weather was nice, and I really didn't feel like going back to the office. Like every other true Londoner, I had major FOMO if I wasn't sitting in a park, drinking champagne and eating strawberries ten minutes after the first sight of sun. I decided to call Emma. My Emma, not Ms Crawford, who was going to be my new assistant, but simply, my sweet Emma. She worked on Mondays, Wednesdays, and Thursdays, but I felt like I had to see her. I think I missed her.

"Hello?" she whispered down the phone, clearly confused why I was calling her during the day.

"Guten Morgen, my dear. What are you doing?"

"I'm at work. Are you okay? What's wrong?"

"Nothing is wrong, sweet-E." I was chuffed on so many levels with the pet name I had just come up with for her because it sounded like sweetie, sweet tea, sweet pea, but it also meant sweet Emma. She may have hidden it, but I knew she had to be impressed, too. "Have you had lunch?"

"No."

"Splendid. Jump in a taxi, and come and meet me. I have planned lunch for us in the park." I hadn't, but she didn't know that.

"I can't, I'm at work."

"Come on. You're always saying that we don't do anything. Now is the time. I need to see you."

"What's come over you?" she asked.

It was a fair question that I didn't really have the answer to. A break, a change of scenery after spending three consecutive days with the guys could have been it, but who knew. "Don't ask questions. Jump in a black cab and meet me at Hyde Park in thirty minutes. Just tell your boss you're not feeling well. Lady stuff. I'm waiting." I hung up the phone before she had a chance to talk herself out of it. I was a little surprised by my spontaneity myself. I guess, I had learned something good from Max after all.

I had her, so all I needed was the picnic. The closest supermarket I could think of, which wasn't a Tesco Metro, was the M&S by Green Park. As I started walking up Piccadilly, I saw Fortnum & Mason. Perfect! I only went there when I had friends or family visiting from abroad, but I knew they did great hampers and would have everything I needed to make my impromptu picnic in the park plot come together. I spent about eight hundred pounds on the basket, a blanket, champagne, and snacks, but it was totally worth it. This was all of a sudden turning into something a lot bigger than I had imagined. I wasn't going to propose to her, but I was going to open up to her for the first time. I had spent weeks pushing her away and being cold, not always intentionally, but subconsciously because I knew it wouldn't last. Something had changed so I had some major making up to do.

When I saw a message from her, my first thought was that she texted to cancel, but she was letting me know that she had arrived at the park. I was still a way off, so I told her to find a good spot and to drop me a pin.

I jumped out of the taxi by the main gate on Hyde Park Corner. We hadn't really done the park thing together before, so we didn't have our usual meeting point. The bags were starting to get heavy, but I finally saw her sitting on a deck chair under the shade of a giant oak tree overlooking The Serpentine. It was lovely, but I was picturing a quieter spot in the middle of a green flat in the sun. I liked the deck chair idea though, so asked her to drag a couple deeper into the park without the warden seeing. I gave her a big kiss, and then started setting up camp. I announced all the goodies as I unpacked them, "Marc de Champagne truffles because I know how much you like them, actual champagne, biscuits, ham, cheddar, caviar, jam, something called fig cheese, more biscuits..."

She was still a little confused, but I could also see how excited she was. To be honest, I was pretty excited too. At that moment, I didn't care about anyone or anything in the world. My only concern was to make her happy. Everything else just seemed to disappear. We talked, we laughed, we drank, and we drank some more.

"How many dogs do you think you can have before people start thinking you're crazy, or that you're a dog walker?" she asked.

I gave it some thought, "four? No, maybe three. Four max."

"What about cats? How many cats would make me a crazy cat lady?"

"In your case, I don't think you need a single one to achieve that title."

She leapt over and slapped my arm. Unable to get a satisfactory contact, she ditched her chair and came to cuddle on mine. I was in a good place. I felt safe, I felt comfortable, I felt happy. It was only that morning that I had questioned our relationship, but the answer was that I liked her, and I liked that she was sweet. She was kind, and loving, and a bit goofy. I hadn't really met a girl I would attribute those qualities to before, so I was playing catch up.

When the sun started to set and it wasn't as warm anymore, we decided to pack up and go back to mine.

"Actually, I should just go home. I can't stay over anyway because I have work tomorrow, and I'm technically closer to my place," she punched.

"No, you're not," I blocked. "Take tomorrow off. We can wake up late, go for brunch, come back to the park." I wasn't ready to let our newly reignited affair end.

"I can't take another day off. You can come to mine if you really want"

Gee, I thought. Her invitation didn't sound very inviting. After such a lovely afternoon, I was a little puzzled why she was being so cold. Plus, I really didn't like going to hers. She lived in a small fourth-floor apartment on Oakley Street. There was a lot more space at mine, and I liked having all my things. "Come on, it will be fun. We need this," I said, conscious not to sound too pushy, "We can jump on a couple of Boris bikes and we'll be there in less than ten minutes."

"Boris bikes? With all this stuff?"

That, to me, was practically a yes. "Sure. Most of this is for the bin anyway. You pack up here, and I'll go and get us some wheels." I paced away as fast as I could, trying to judge whether the docking station on Knightsbridge or Park Lane was nearer.

When I returned with the bikes, she stood there squinting and shielding herself from the piercing sun that glistened on the corner of her face. I felt a little scared that the image in front of me was what my whole life would look like, not because I didn't like it, but because it would be the same forever. I shook the feeling away, to worry about it another day.

She had consolidated everything into one bag and the wicker basket. I hung the bag on the handlebar and balanced the basket on the front of the bike, using the elastic bungee cord thingy to secure it. We were set to go. She went on ahead, but my uneven load coupled with the grassy terrain presented a bit more of a challenge than I had expected. I peddled harder, to get control of the front wheel, but failed and fell flat on my side, metres away from where we were sitting. She came rushing back in a panic to see if I was okay. My bum hurt a little, but my ego took the biggest bruising.

She helped me up, "Too much champagne?"

"Not at all," I replied, a little annoyed and a little embarrassed. It was emasculating that she thought I couldn't handle my drink. If only she knew the amount I had consumed at Cali's party the night before, but I thought it probably best not to mention that.

She continued to show concern, "Are you sure you're okay? Do you want to sit down for a bit? Shall I get us a taxi?" I was fine, but her mothering made it more dramatic than it needed to be. A part of me wished that she was the type of girl that could have just laughed it off.

# MAX

Thursday night really was the best for first dates. It was close enough to the weekend that she wouldn't be stressed out by work, but still far enough that you could actually go somewhere nice without it being overrun by yobs on a night out-out. I say that, but there wasn't really ever a quiet night during the summer in London.

I was rather looking forward to it. The first Bumble girl had gone quiet on me, but Laura looked even hotter in her bikini photo. Sounds shallow, I know, but wasn't the whole concept of online dating a little shallow? I mean, there wasn't a whole lot to go on. She preferred the beach over mountains, she enjoyed both nights in watching Netflix and nights out clubbing, and I knew that she would rather be rich than famous, but that was about it.

She wanted to meet for a drink after work at a place near her office, but I insisted we do dinner. I may have played that game with girls in the past, but I wasn't willing to be played like that. I had to start by making it explicitly clear that the date wasn't a casual rendezvous she could fit in on her way home, the same way she might stop off at the supermarket to pick up groceries for dinner that evening. It was an event in itself. There was going to be no safety net of being able to end it after a drink or two. It had to be official, formal, dangerous, frighteningly awkward if it must. I was going old school with it. I even asked for her address so that I could pick her up. Unfortunately, that bit didn't go to plan, and she insisted that she'd meet me at the restaurant. You can't win 'em all, I suppose. I hadn't been to Hide on Piccadilly since it opened, and it was the first place that popped into my head for some reason, so I made a reservation for eight thirty. That gave her enough time to go home after work and get ready for the date. I spent the whole day prepping. I went for a haircut, made sure my favourite shirt was dry cleaned, and did some manscaping just in case. I was looking and feeling sharp.

I did my usual routine of getting to the restaurant at least twenty minutes early to make sure I got a nice, private table in the corner. My worst nightmare was standing around awkwardly with someone I'd just met, waiting to be seated. I folded four twenty-pound notes and kept them ready in my pocket for greasing the host, the waiter, and anyone else who came in the way. It wasn't one of my regular haunts, so it really helped to make sure we'd get extra special service. The first order on the agenda was a bottle of Bruni Paillard Cuvee 72 champagne. The trick was, order the champagne before she arrived so that she wouldn't know I went for one closer to the top of the list. The problem was, I had gotten through a whole bottle before she had arrived. I hoped she was running late. I guess, my worst nightmare was actually being stood up. I must have checked my phone and refreshed my messages every five seconds, but there was nothing from her. I waited patiently and was willing to overlook her tardiness, reminding myself how good she looked in a bikini.

She did eventually come rushing over, thirty-seven minutes late. "I'm sorry, there was a lot of traffic. I hate Central London," she huffed while taking off her coat and sitting down.

It all happened so fast that I didn't have a chance to properly introduce myself and greet her how I had planned to. Before we got to formalities, the waiter came over to offer her water.

"A bottle of Dom Perignon please, Moe" I kindly ordered. Luckily, it still sat in the middle of the list and was far from the more expensive options, but it had brand appeal, so she could tell her friends about it the next day.

She didn't react to the order or the fact that I had learned the waiter's name. The next thing I noticed about her was that she made zero effort to dress up. Her makeup hadn't been retouched, her hair hadn't been reworked, her nails were chipped, and her attitude made me feel like the date was a chore. I tried to judge whether it was inexperience, or if she had been on so many app dates that she had given up caring. "It's nice to meet you, how's your day going?" I asked.

"Shit. Work was crap. I went out for drinks with my boss before this, and he was being a right tool."

The waiter filled our flutes and replaced the bottle in the bucket by our table. I raised my glass, "Well, champagne always makes me feel better." Nothing. I broke the long silence after the cheers with, "I know these are sometimes so weird, but why don't you tell me more about yourself. I know you prefer beaches over mountains, but what kind of stuff are you into?"

"Like hobbies?"

Did she think I meant sexually? I wanted to know, but, "Yes."

"Umm, I don't know. Just normal things," she said slowly.

It was harder than I had hoped. "What do you consider normal?"

While perusing the menu, "I like music."

"Everyone likes music. Any particular artist or genre?"

"I like a bit of everything."

Ah, there it was. The dreaded answer most people without any personality gave when asked about music. "What are you listening to these days?"

"Mostly EDM. I like harder stuff, too."

I didn't know much about EDM, so I had to think where I could carry the conversation next because it was becoming more and more clear that she wasn't interested in taking part in the evening. "Have you been away recently or have any travel plans coming up?" That was always a classic.

"Why?" she asked, moving from the menu to her phone.

I wasn't sure whether she was talking to me, but I answered anyway, "Just wondering. Do you like to travel much?"

Still looking at her phone, she replied, "Oh, yeah, I went to Spain last month with the girls and will probably go again later this year."

The more she spoke, the less attractive she became. I pointed to her wrist, "Cool, I see you have a tattoo. What does it say?" It was a reach, but I was running thin.

She looked at it and read, "Good vibes."

"Cool, cool." I was aware I was saying the word *cool* a lot, but needed it to fill the gaps between my follow-ups. The conversation was flowing like a pond. "Do you have any more?"

"Tattoos? Yeah, I have most of my back covered."

Didn't see that in any of her photos. I liked a cute butterfly, or heart, or something small and girly on the back of the neck, or behind the ear, on the foot, or on the shoulder, but the whole back seemed a little much. "With what?"

"Just random stuff."

Her vague replies were tiring, and it didn't get any better. By the end of the main course, I was exhausted. Finishing off my champagne, I hesitantly asked, "Dessert?"

"I have to get back because this place is such a nightmare to get to."

More like, wherever she lived was a nightmare to go to. I thought about offering to get her an Uber and escorting her home, but decided against it. She would have confused the kind gesture with something else, so I saved myself the rejection.

As I signalled the waiter for the bill, she got up to leave. "Thank you so much for dinner. It was really nice. I better get going if I want to catch the train. Bye." Quick and painless. She walked off, likely never to be heard from again.

# HUGO

Emma and I ended up spending the rest of the week together. She went to her place to pick up some clothes on the Thursday and I popped into work for a bit on Friday morning, but apart from that, we stayed in to Amazon Prime Video and chill. We were getting on really well. There were times when I would, out of habit, start thinking about all the reasons why it couldn't, and wouldn't work out between us, but, for once, I fought the feeling and thought of all the reasons why it should. It might not have been the healthiest approach, and I was aware that those things would likely come back to haunt me when I was a lot deeper in, but that was the strategy I had chosen.

We were in the fast lane, so the next natural step was for her to meet the gang. I mean, she had already met Max a few times here and there and had briefly been introduced to Will and Cali at an event when we first started going out, but we never had a chance to all hang out together. I say all;

I thought it would be safer to start with just Max and Will. Cali was sometimes a bit much to take. He was an acquired taste, but once you got to know him, he had a heart of gold. Still, his reputation definitely preceded him and she wasn't too fond of what she'd heard. Baby steps. She was also a little unsure of Max. She'd only met him after we'd both had a bit to drink, so there was some mending there to do, too.

Sunday roast at The Coach Makers Arms on Marylebone Lane sounded ideal. I didn't get much of a chance to prep the lads on what to say, or more importantly, what not to say, but I knew they'd be on their best behaviour. I was looking forward to it, but was also, unexpectedly, a little nervous.

Max was already on his second pint when we arrived but had a cold one waiting for me and a glass of white wine already poured for Emma.

"How did you know I'd want a white wine?" she asked.

"It's a special talent Max has. He always knows what drink to order for people," I answered for him.

"Not so much a talent than a gift or a superpower," Max joked. "Lovely to see you again, Emma."

I raised my glass and took a sip before I sat down. "Dankeschön for the beer, mate"

Emma tried hers and praised Max's choice. "I suppose it is, but how do you… What if I wanted —"

Not giving her a chance to finish, Max explained, "Then you would have made the wrong decision. You would have considered an Aperol spritz, or a mojito, maybe. You would have looked over the wine list, but when the waiter asked, you would have panicked and gone for a G&T." He was in his element, so I didn't interrupt and looked over the menu. "Now, even if you did go for white wine, you would have asked for the waiter's recommendation, which would have been an even bigger mistake. There was no question that you needed a full-bodied chardonnay from Burgundy because, although you'd usually go for the turbot, we'd all go for the ultimate roast, so there was a chance that you'd give in to the peer pressure and do the same. Either way, you went, the wine in your glass pairs perfectly, and you wouldn't have the stress of changing drinks halfway through."

A little cocky, but spot on. He waited for Emma's reaction. It could have gone either way really. She could have found it presumptuous or condescending, but she was impressed too. "Well, cheers again to that," I toasted.

Will arrived, apologising for being late. He gave me a hug and formally introduced himself to Emma.

"Got you a water, old chap" Max stated.

"Perfect, just what I needed. Thank you."

Max shot Emma a smug little smile, which forced her to giggle and relax.

The waiter came over to take our orders, "Are you ready?"

"I still need a few minutes. You can start with them," said Emma.

"Ultimate roast for me," I ordered.

"Oooh, that sounds good. I'll go for that too," added Will.

Max, pretended to ponder, but finally followed suit, "Make that three. Emma, you're back in the hot seat."

"Fine, I give in, I'll do the same."

"Attagirl."

Will didn't stay long after lunch as he had a concert to get to, but Emma still had quite a bit of wine left, so Max and I ordered another round of beers. Max and Will were always team Emma, but it felt really nice that Emma was now also Team Max and Will. Either that, or she was a very good actress and I'd hear about it later.

"So, how's your friend, Millie was it?" Max asked, trying to sound as genuine as possible, but I knew exactly why he was asking.

"It was, and she's fine thanks," Emma answered. I think she also knew why he was asking, but didn't humour him with any further information.

What she didn't know was that it wouldn't discourage him in any way, "She's very pretty. Is she —"

Emma cut him off, "I'm not going to set you up with her."

"Why not?"

"Well, first of all, she's kind of seeing someone, and second, I really like her and we're good friends, so if you two broke up, it would be awkward. I never set people up."

Both valid points, but no surprise they were unsatisfactory for Max. "First, 'kind of seeing someone' doesn't sound very serious or promising, and second, why are you assuming we would break up? What if we were to get married, have children, and live happily ever after? Why would you deny her that?"

"I don't know…" Emma forfeited, "Just go on Tinder."

"Yeah, what happened to that Bumble girl," I asked.

"Long story."

"Well, luckily, Emma still has half a bottle of wine to get through, thanks to you."

"I can't finish the whole bottle," Emma exclaimed. "Well, maybe I could. You got the drink right, Max, but you didn't take into consideration that I was a slow drinker."

"Maybe I did, otherwise you guys would have left straight after lunch," Max replied.

"Touché, but seriously what happened?"

He got comfortable in his seat, took a sip of beer, and started, "Well, the one I told you about must have died because I didn't hear from her ever again, but I matched with someone even hotter." As soon as he said that, he looked at Emma to apologise for being boorish. "Thursday night. I got all dressed up. I offered to pick her up, but she refused and said she'd meet me at the restaurant. Whatever. I took her to Hide on Piccadilly, ordered a bottle of champagne — "

Emma was already hooked into the story, "Why champagne?"

"Because we were going to celebrate the start of something special and that's how I roll on dates," he boasted as if he was expecting the question. "She turned up nearly forty minutes late. She came in complaining. She didn't make any effort to dress up. She said the food was pretentious. She didn't ask me a single question. She didn't even offer to go Dutch."

"Would you have let her pay half?" I questioned, full well knowing he wouldn't have.

"No, but she could have at least offered. And worst of all, she was on her phone the whole night. 'Twas a right bore. I'm done with app dating."

I actually felt bad for the poor fella. He could be very particular and extremely picky, but the stuff he described was the bare minimum that you'd expect. "Shame. Sounds like a bad egg, but you shouldn't give up."

"The pool has really dried up. I feel like Tinder is for kids looking to hook up, nobody really uses Happn anymore, and the girls on Bumble never like or message me."

"Maybe it's your profile. Show Emma. Maybe a girl's perspective is just what you need," I suggested.

Max hesitantly pulled out his phone, opened Tinder and handed it to Emma. She scrolled through, carefully examining every element. "You're too far away in your main photo. You need a clear photo so that the girl can actually see your face. And you should be smiling."

"I don't like to smile in photos. I don't even like to take photos. I mean, who even takes photos anymore apart from Instagram models?"

"You don't have any photos with friends either. You should have one group photo at the end so that she knows you're social. And one of you doing something cool like hiking outdoors." She obviously knew what she was talking about. "Also, you should write more about yourself in your bio. The bio is like the most important part. Just be honest, funny, and maybe ask a question."

"Ugh! Is that all? I'm so done with all these rules. Can't I just meet someone in real life? Is that too much to ask?"

Out of nowhere, Belle, Max's dog, came running over to greet him. I'd never seen Max happier than when he was with her. It's like he became a different person. Emma lit up too, and quickly took the initiative to take a snap of them. Belle then came running around to our side of the table and started licking my hand.

"Hello, Belle," I said in my best baby voice.

Max's dog sitter, who I hadn't really met or heard much about, wasn't far behind. "Hey, Max. I'm so sorry. I hope you don't mind. I had Belle, and then came in here to meet someone for a drink, but he cancelled, and I was about to leave, but then Belle saw you..."

"Of course not. Join us. You've met my friend Hugo before, and this is Emma."

I was glad I didn't have to introduce Emma. I wouldn't have known what to say. I wanted to call her my girlfriend, but there were new rules about that. I would have needed to sit down with Max to chat about it first. Oh, and Emma too, I suppose. Girlfriend. It sounded so official. It also sounded like we were back in secondary school. Partner? That sounded like we were in business together. My girl or my woman were too possessive. My lover? What, were we in a Mills & Boon novel?

Fluttering her words, "Oh, no, I couldn't. Lovely to meet you. I can take Belle and drop her off later this evening if you want."

"Nonsense. You're joining us. You're already here and you were going to stay for a drink anyway." Max could be very persuasive. He pulled out the chair he was leaning on, "Hugo, Emma, this is Holly. She's a friend, a lifesaver, and like a mother to Belle." He got the attention of our waiter, "French 75, please."

"What's that?" Holly asked

"You'll like it," he said, confidently.

Holly looked at Emma, who reassured her, "It's a gift he has apparently."

"So, what were you guys talking about?"

It was my turn to get back at him, "Max here was telling us about his gross misfortunes in the world of app dating," I reported.

"Don't even get me started. I was supposed to meet a guy from Tinder here, and he totally bailed at the last minute," Holly shared, saving Max any embarrassment.

"What a twit," he bursted angrily.

"Thanks," Holly guessed, a little unsure about exactly what Max meant by his tone. "Are you two together?" She asked Emma and I.

Americans were so forward. I shuffled apprehensively on my chair and fidgeted with my glass.

Emma looked at me and jumped in, "Ignore him. He's still a bit of a child with these things sometimes. Yes, we're together, but we haven't really had that talk about official labels yet," she affirmed, confidently.

Her true personality, which Max hadn't really witnessed until then, was starting to shine through, and I had never been more attracted to her. Sweet, sweet Emma could also take control when she needed to.

"That's awesome," Holly said, appreciating the honesty.

Feeling a little left out of the conversation, and hoping to prevent it from going back to his relationship status, Max announced, "Holly's at Regent's doing Enterprise & Innovation."

"Now that's awesome. That's where Max and I went. It's a part of the Global Management series, right?" Unlike Max, I had stayed in touch with our alma mater and had even given a couple of talks at alumni events.

"Hugo owns a pretty innovative enterprise himself," Max bragged. He always made it out to be a lot bigger and better than it was, but I appreciated it. "In fact, you're still hiring for an assistant, right? Maybe Holly could intern for you?"

"Really? That would be amazing. I'd definitely be interested," she expressed.

I didn't know how to tell them that I had already hired someone without sounding rude. Even if I hadn't, I didn't feel comfortable hiring friends or friends of friends for similar reasons to Emma not wanting to hook Max up with

Millie. "Actually, I've already kind of filled that position, but will keep you posted if —"

"What! You didn't tell me," Max clamoured. Composing himself, "Was it the other Emma? Please tell me it was the other Emma."

I hadn't told my Emma about the other Emma. I don't know why, but I felt a little guilty. It was like I was cheating on her with a work Emma that just happened to be a hot redhead that I'd be spending most of my day with. Nothing had happened, and nothing would, but Max definitely wasn't helping the situation. "We're still waiting to finalise everything," was the best I had. Luckily, the waiter interrupted with Holly's drink.

Her eyes widened. As she took a sip, we all leaned in, waiting for her verdict, "Wow! That's delicious. What is it?"

Max, smug as ever, "French 75. Gin, champagne, lemon, and a little bit of sugar."

"I would never have ordered that. I've never even heard of it. I would have just gotten another gin and tonic." As she said that, I saw Emma raise her eyebrows and nod her head towards Max out of respect. He just sat there grinning like a Cheshire cat.

I was tired. As much as I liked having Emma over at mine, I slept a lot better when I was alone. So much so, that I sometimes wondered if I'd ever want to get married or live with anyone. I valued my independence and freedom. Emma had planned to return to hers after the pub, so I was eager to go home and enjoy the few hours of the weekend I had left. Without any fair warning, I downed the rest of my pint and stood up to leave. "Thanks for coming, Max." I leaned down to give Belle a big cuddle. "It was really lovely to see you again, Holly."

Emma, caught a little off guard, mirrored and followed me out.

# MAX

"Why did they leave so suddenly?" Holly asked. "Was it because of me?"

"Not at all. It's a thing Hugo has started doing recently. He thinks about leaving secretly in his head, and then when he's ready, he quickly pulls the trigger. It helps him leave when he should because he's terribly easy to persuade otherwise."

"That's odd," Holly remarked.

"You don't know the half of it." I had known Holly for the good part of a year, but we'd never actually sat down and chatted much. It was always a brief encounter in passing when she picked up or dropped off Belle. And yet, I trusted her with the keys to my house. "I'm sure you have some odd friends."

"Excuse me? And why is that?"

"You look like the type that attracts them," I ribbed. "You know I didn't mean it like that. I meant, everyone has eccentric friends."

"I know. Yeah, a few, but they're all in the US."

"Of course they are." I was on a roll. "You're from Ohio, no, Iowa, right? I always get those two mixed up for some reason."

"Yes, a small town not too far from Cedar Rapids"

"Sounds like a ride at Thorpe Park."

Whenever she was confused, she scrunched her nose, as if she was displeased or cross about something. "Thorpe Park?"

"It's a theme park." It felt only natural to follow that with an invitation to go, but I had to remind myself that we hardly knew each other. Plus, I hated rides. "Have you made a good group of friends here in London?" I asked, sincerely.

"Not really." She actually looked a little sad and frustrated about it. "It's just so hard to meet people. Especially in a big city where no one talks to anyone. That's why I joined Tinder, but I don't think I'll be using that anymore."

"Yeah, Tinder probably isn't the best place to make friends. What about the people on your course?"

"You know what they're like. They seem to all already know each other and stick to their little cliques. You have the Chinese group, the Arabic group, and the Russians, who just go out partying most of the time. Not really my thing. No offence."

"Why would I be offended? It was a little different when we were there. What is your thing?"

"I like being outdoors, I like dogs, I like going to galleries."

"Is that what it says on your Tinder profile?" I jested.

Not wanting to admit it, "Maybe." Wanting to change the subject, "Is Hugo your best friend?"

"Yes. I mean, I don't know. Guys don't really have best friends. There's four of us in total. Will was here earlier, I think you also met him once briefly, and then there's Cali."

"What's wrong with Cali? You said his name in a way that indicates that you're not really sure about him."

"There's nothing wrong with him, he's just a little extra, shall we say. That's why he wasn't here today." Her nose reminded me that she wasn't aware of why I was there. "That was the all-important 'Meet your friend's new girlfriend' lunch." It appeared that I had to spell it out before she loosened her expression, "You know, when your friend starts going out with someone new, you have to arrange a lunch so everyone can get to know each other."

"No, I didn't know that was a thing. Well, I knew it was a thing, but I didn't know it was an official thing. Wait, did I crash an official thing?" She said in quick succession.

"It's fine. It was nice you got to meet them. We can be your first official friends in London."

"Great!" she said with sarcased enthusiasm. "Well?"

A little offended, "What, are we too old?"

"No," she clarified, "I meant, well, what did you think of her?"

"Oh, I had met her before. I really like her. I think she's great for Hugo. Will and I have been encouraging him and are in full support of the courtship."

She racked her brain, "Will, I can't remember meeting him."

"Don't worry, not many people do."

"That's not very nice to say about your friend."

"I'm only joking, but he is a little dull. Although, he's in a bit of a bind because he kissed Cali's sister on a night out earlier this week." I don't know why I told her that. Maybe it was the alcohol, or maybe it was the fact that I'd been meaning to talk to Hugo about it, and it slipped my mind. I needed somebody to gossip with.

She found it interesting. "Whoa! Isn't that like against guy code or something?"

"What do you know about guy code? But, yes. Thing is, he didn't know it was his sister when he kissed, and fell in love with her." I was very aware that I sounded like a sixteen-year-old girl spreading rumours in the playground. "Now he doesn't know what to do. And I don't know why I'm telling you this."

"It's okay, I won't tell anyone. I have no one to tell," she self-deprecated in a very British way. "So, what is he going to do? Did Cali find out? Was he pissed? Did Cali say, 'Marry my sister or I'm going to punch you?' What kind of a name is Cali anyway? Wait, was it like when Chandler kissed Joey's sister in *Friends*?"

Her excitement excited me. I laughed, "No, it wasn't like *Friends*. It was better. We were at breakfast and when Cali found out, he stormed off. Okay, maybe not as dramatic as it sounds, but you had to be there. I don't know. I think he really likes her."

"Then he should tell Cali that. If Will and Cali are good friends then Cali should be happy his sister gets to date a good guy." Sound and sensible advice.

"Do you have any brothers or sisters?" I asked.

"I have a younger brother."

"Would you let him date one of your friends?"

She thought about it for less than a second before exhibiting her disgust, "Ew, no. Gross! But he's a lot younger."

"I think she's a lot younger, too."

"Yeah, but it's different for guys."

I agreed. Everyone knew the French rule—half your age plus seven—but I didn't say it out loud because Holly just fell out of the bottom bracket of my parameter and I didn't want to reinforce a rule that wasn't in my favour. Not that anything would ever happen between us. Sure, I thought she was pretty pretty and I'd be lying if I said I hadn't thought about it on more than one occasion. I usually knew within seven-tenths of a second of seeing a girl whether I would sleep with her, but I wasn't exaggerating when I said Holly was a lifesaver. I honestly would have been lost without her. I had made peace with the fact that our relationship would remain professional—dog owner and dog sitter. Plus, she was too young. She still had a lot of life to live, a lot of places to go, a lot of hearts to break... The more I told myself that, the more I believed it. Truth was, if I thought I had a shot, I would have taken it. "Have you ever dated a younger guy? Or what's the oldest you've dated?" I slipped in.

"My last proper boyfriend that I actually went out with was a few months younger than me, but I prefer older guys because they're usually a bit more mature."

I begged to disagree, but there was a lot more pressing information in her comment. The headlines read that she was open to casual flings and that maybe I did have a chance.

"My flatmate is dating a guy who's forty-five. It's kind of gross and I'm sure he is married," she said with a lot of judgement.

Maybe I didn't. "Sugar daddy?"

Her tone turning to envy, "Yes, he's basically paying all of her tuition and rent, and buying her all these expensive bags and shoes all the time. The money she gets from her parents, she spends on travelling and going out." She paused and looked at Belle, "Do you ever wonder what she's thinking or how much she understands of what's going on in the world?" Holly jumped from topic to topic, ignoring the rules of regular conversations. In a way, it exuded comfort and confidence in her being.

I caught Belle's eye as I answered, "All the time. Dogs are supposed to be smart, right? But how smart? Does she know the concept of friends, relationships, money, the stresses we go through in our daily lives?" The rhythm of my speech began to mimic hers.

"You don't have any stresses."

Maybe they were all first world problems, but they were still problems.

Still locked into Belle, "She's started doing things like pretending to dig after she's done a poo, even if it's on the sidewalk, and eating her food away from her bowl. I read those are all hard-wired traits in some breeds. The whole pack mentality."

"Yeah, I noticed that, too, but thought that she was just being weird. Do you think people are born with instincts?" I was pleased that we were getting deeper.

"Of course, that's how we survive," she said with substance.

"I don't know. I think most things, if not everything, is a learned response."

"Some people are naturally talented at things. Look at you, you have a natural talent for painting. You can't learn that," she fired back.

There was a compliment in there, but I disagreed with her on both fronts. "Thank you, but I really don't. I think you can learn anything. You just need to spend ten thousand hours on something and you're good to go."

"Yeah, but you could get two people who both spend the same time on something and one would naturally be better at it."

"Nurturally, not naturally. There's no way of really testing it."

"Well, I disagree, but I do think your work is cool. How come you don't show it more?"

"I sometimes feel like I'm not artisty enough. I'm not out there. I don't have pink hair, or wear funny clothes, or fit the typical mould of an artist." It was the first time I had really opened up or answered the question aloud but it seemed to come flooding out.

"Maybe not a struggling artist, but successful artists were all members of high society." Her voice was calm, considered, and comforting.

I never looked at it like that. "True, but who'd want to see my work anyway?"

"I would," she exclaimed. "I've only seen a few half-finished pieces at your place. You never post your stuff on Instagram. You really need to post your stuff on Instagram."

"Picasso didn't post his stuff on Instagram," I squabbled.

"That's because Instagram didn't exist. I'm sure Gertrude Stein would have been the biggest influencer of her day." Her words were twined with sophistication, intelligence, and humour, which I found surprising for a girl in her early twenties. "You have to make use of what you have been gifted with. I'll help you set up an Instagram account for your work. I wish I could paint."

"Everyone can paint," I objected.

"I wouldn't know what to paint. I wouldn't even know where to begin, what paint to use, or how to mix them, or even what tools I would need?"

"All you need is something to paint with and something to paint on. The rest just kind of takes over and happens," I said like a true artist.

"Do I buy oil paints, acrylics, or watercolours?"

"All that stuff is a personal decision and depends on the style you choose. I work with oils mostly."

"Will you teach me the basics?"

"Sure, anytime," I offered.

"How about now?" she asked, eagerly.

I didn't know what to say. An offer usually stopped with the invitation. She wasn't supposed to take it literally. It was just supposed to be one of those things we talked about, but never actually got around to doing. I felt like I was being held to account, but I couldn't think of a good enough reason not to, so I checked, "Like, now-now?"

"Yeah! I mean, if you're not busy. You can show me what I need to buy to get started, so I can go to Cass Art and stock up on supplies tomorrow."

I didn't know what the rush was, but I liked her follow through. "I have some stuff I don't really use that much anymore that you can have to start with."

"Really? That would be so amazing. So, can we go now to get it?" she pushed.

"I don't see why not." I finished off my pint as she walked Belle out.

# SCENE FOURTEEN

It was the perfect summer evening and the sky was still a lovely shade of cobalt blue when we got back to my place. Belle immediately ran to her spot underneath the kitchen table and settled in. Every few weeks, she claimed a new patch where she spent all of her time until she got tired of it and moved onto the next. For some reason, she preferred the hardwood floor over the plush dog bed I had bought her. I walked over to my spot, the bar, and poured myself three fingers of Scotch. "Can I get you anything?" I asked as a formality, already walking around the counter.

Surprisingly, "Sure."

I was sure she would kindly decline. "What can I get you?"

"Well, you should know, shouldn't you?"

Touché. I scrambled through the ingredients in front of me in a bit of a panic. I pulled out a shaker and started improvising. I had recently gotten into mixology, so was more than thrilled to be put to the test. A bit of vodka, some lime juice, ice... I was halfway to a Cosmo, so I threw in some Cointreau, but I didn't have any cranberry juice so I muddled some raspberries and started shaking for dramatic effect. I held back on cracking a Tom Cruise in *Cocktail* joke, because the reference, and probably Tom Cruise for that matter, were before her time. Still a little off with the quantity, I poured half of the shaker into a fancy cocktail glass through a strainer, and dumped the rest in the sink. I garnished with a raspberry and a leaf of mint to watch her eyes widen once more.

"What's this?"

"It's a Raspbopolitan."

"Looks, yummy."

Satisfied with my concoction, I walked her to the guest bedroom, which I had transformed into my studio to keep visitors from visiting.

She waltzed in and started commenting on the many paintings that lined the room. Suddenly, she stopped and pulled out her phone to take a photo.

"OMG! I love this one! How —"

I never felt so vulnerable. I ushered her away. The piece was unfinished and one I wasn't particularly proud of. I pointed to a pile of blank canvases stacked up in the corner.

"Pick a couple of any size you want, and I'll dismantle one of these easels for you. Don't worry, I'll walk it over to yours so that you don't have to carry it."

"Wait, aren't you going to teach me how to paint first?" she asked ever so politely.

"There's really nothing to it."

She continued to animatically bat her eyelids, "Please?"

I took one of my paintings down and signalled for her to pass me a fresh board. She hopped at the opportunity.

"How do you get in the zone? Do you have any rituals? I was watching this show, and the guy is a writer, and before he starts writing, he has to do a series of things like a special pose, and eat almonds, and take a shot of port…" she drifted.

I found her pleniloquence rather endearing. I squeezed out some paint on a palette as she carefully selected a paintbrush like she was a nurse prepping to hand a doctor a scalpel during a Hollywood operation. "So, you take some paint on your brush, you mix it with a medium to control the density and how fast it dries, and then you put it on the canvas. I told you there was nothing to it. All you have to remember is, paint fat over lean."

"Okay, I know what all of those words mean, but I have no idea what you mean. So, where do you get your inspiration from?"

Where did I get my inspiration from? It was a good question. "I listen to music while I paint."

"What kind of music?" she asked?

I was about to fall into my own trap and say a little bit of everything, but stopped myself just in time. "I like the old classics. Elvis, Sinatra. Love a bit of Meat Loaf."

"'I'd Do Anything For Love' is one of my favourite songs ever."

I was impressed. "How do you know about Meat Loaf? Your generation doesn't know good music."

"We have the best music. Taylor Swift is a goddess," she cheered. "I also love country."

I didn't know much about either, but it was refreshing to see how passionately she answered. "It's all just mumble rap and Justin Bieber saying 'Yummy, yummy' over and over again these days. Good music is dead," I argued. I recalled my dad saying the same to me when I went through my West Coast gangster rap phase in the 90s.

"That's. So. Not. True!" she squawked.

I handed her the palette and brush. "Here, you give it a go."

She nervously stepped into position in front of the canvas.

"If you can't twerk to it on TikTok, it's not making the charts these days," I continued.

She turned over her shoulder, shook her head, and stuck her tongue out at me. She turned back and clumsily stabbed the brush against the canvas, making short, patchy streaks. She went for more paint, but, again, it didn't last long.

"You're pressing too hard," I instructed.

She shrugged her shoulders out of frustration, as she tried again.

I placed my hand over hers, which was somehow already covered in paint, and slowly moved it up the handle, loosening her grip. I guided it to the palette, lifted some Liquin, mixed it with a deep cadmium red, and brought it back up to the canvas. I gently placed the bristles to the cotton and moved down to make a smooth, even stroke. She turned her head, looked up at me with her bright blue eyes, and smiled. We kissed.

# CREDITS